He couldn't think of anything he wanted more than for Jasmine to spend the rest of the night with him.

"Need to go?" he finally asked.

Jasmine hesitated. If he'd been in her situation, he would have, too.

Covering the few steps left between them, Royce let his body act on instinct. He reached out and cupped the cool skin of her upper arms. Then he rubbed up and down, aiming to warm her. But also to fulfill his own craving to simply touch her.

She stared up at him in the dark. Beneath his touch, she shivered, then she shook her head no.

"Then come back to bed."

That first touch of skin on skin exhilarated him. He rolled over her in the bed, covering her cool body with his warmth. Savoring the gasp of air that signaled her surrender.

* * *

A Family for the Billionaire is part of Harlequin Desire's #1 bestselling series, Billionaires and Babies: Powerful men...wrapped around their babies' little fingers.

Dear Reader,

I've had the privilege of visiting the fascinating city of Savannah, Georgia, and it was well worth the travel time with its old-world charm, mysterious histories and gorgeous architecture.

It's the perfect setting for my new series featuring a trio of Southern sisters—these young women have overcome a lot of heartache and adversity. They've worked hard to keep their family together, and now they will each grow their family circle by finding love in the most unexpected ways.

Join me as I explore this city filled with Southern charm and contemporary commerce with the first Harden sister, Jasmine, as she transforms the heart of her CEO in *A Family for the Billionaire*.

I love to hear from my readers! You can email me at readdaniwade@gmail.com, or follow me on Facebook. As always, news about my releases is easiest to find through my author newsletter, which you can sign up for from my website at www.daniwade.com.

Enjoy!

Dani

DANI WADE

A FAMILY FOR THE BILLIONAIRE

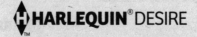

Recycling programs
for this product may
not exist in your area.

ISBN-13: 978-0-373-83866-0

A Family for the Billionaire

HARLEQUIN®

™www.Harlequin.com

Printed in U.S.A.

Dani Wade astonished her local librarians as a teenager when she carried home ten books every week—and actually read them all. Now she writes her own characters, who clamor for attention in the midst of the chaos that is her life. Residing in the Southern United States with a husband, two kids, two dogs and one grumpy cat, she stays busy until she can closet herself away with her characters once more.

Books by Dani Wade

Harlequin Desire

His by Design
Reining in the Billionaire
Unbridled Billionaire
A Family for the Billionaire

Milltown Millionaires

A Bride's Tangled Vows
The Blackstone Heir
The Renegade Returns
Expecting His Secret Heir

Visit her Author Profile page at Harlequin.com, or daniwade.com, for more titles.

To all the sisters who have enriched my travels and blessed my life—LeaAnn, Sheridan, Tammy, Hannah, Nicole, Kim, Kira, Andrea, Marilyn, Linda and LJ.

My journeys wouldn't have been the same without you...

One

"I assume this meeting is being conducted with the utmost confidentiality?"

"Of course," Jasmine Harden said, though she had never before had to assure a potential client of that.

"Then I'll be honest."

She eyed Royce Brazier as he paced before her in his suit and tie. The floor-to-ceiling windows of his office overlooked the river and provided the perfect backdrop. Gorgeous—the man and the view. As he paused for a moment, she noticed just a hint of something on his neck, right above his collar in the back. Was that a tattoo?

Quickly Jasmine dropped her gaze. She knew exactly how easy it was to read her expression, so she turned her thoughts in more businesslike directions.

"Besides," he continued as he faced her once more, "if word got out, I'd know where it came from, wouldn't I?"

Okay, Royce was making it a lot easier to focus on business.

"My shipping fleet has done very well, but I'm interested in taking my business to a new level. To that end, I'm aiming to attract a certain family that I hope will contract extensive work from my fleet." A frown marred Royce's smooth forehead. She could almost see the thoughts as they took hold of him. "This family is very altruistic and so I want to do a fund-raising event that appeals to them."

"So this is all about a business deal?" Though she could understand the logic Royce was working with, the conclusion was still disappointing. The hot CEO apparently didn't have a heart…

"It's purely a business endeavor. As with other projects, I'll write the check, you do the work."

Wasn't that a nice attitude? Not. Though Jasmine regularly worked with high-profile businessmen in this city, she'd never had one approach her with a proposal this cold. "Why me?" she asked quietly.

"I did my research," he said, turning a direct stare on her that made her uncomfortably aware of things other than business. "You're well known in the circles I want to attract, your clients have a very high rate of satisfaction and we use some of the same vendors, the best vendors in the city of Savannah."

His praise should make her feel better, right?

"My assistant received some wonderful feedback on

you. You were rated the highest of star-quality event planners in the region.

"I only work with the best of the best. That's how I can trust you to do the work."

Why did he have to be so handsome? A handsome automaton. That slight peek at a tattoo on his neck had led her to expect more. A huff of laughter escaped as she imagined him as a true robot in her overactive imagination.

"Is there a problem?" he asked, narrowing his eyes on her as if suspicious she was making fun of him.

"Nothing." At least she hadn't giggled. That would definitely be unprofessional. "Can you tell me what charity you have in mind?" she asked, trying to get back on track.

"I don't. Pick whatever you feel is appropriate."

Jasmine blinked. Everything about this meeting was completely out of the ordinary when it came to how she worked with her clients.

"I simply need an event that is noteworthy and appropriate," he continued. "They seem to be involved in quite a few causes. Oh, and I need it in less than two months."

Oh, my. "So you think I'm a miracle worker?"

This time he relented enough to offer a small smile. "I certainly hope so. Otherwise the event will be too late to have any impact on my bid. Can I count on you?"

She thought back over their conversation. No. No. And no. "Listen, I don't think I'm the right person for this job." Or quite frankly, for this boss. She had a feeling that working for him would be a minefield, and with her life in tumult already, she didn't need a difficult boss.

He stopped his pacing to stare. "Why not?"

You're too handsome, too business minded and too cavalier about this endeavor altogether.

Only she couldn't say any of that out loud. Questions rang in Jasmine's mind as she watched him, thinking hard. She'd heard plenty about Royce Brazier, but she'd never actually met him before today, despite her extensive work with Savannah's elite. One of the city's youngest billionaires—self-made through his dedication to his quickly growing shipping business—he attended only a few select events on the social scene. Considering his reputation as a hard-nosed, focused businessman and what she'd seen during this meeting, she had a feeling he only did that much to maintain his business contacts.

His presence was commanding, his look suave and professional. So suave she wanted to mess with his perfectly placed blond hair just for the heck of it. Jasmine was professional, too, but she often had the feeling she was herding cats—especially since the arrival of Rosie…and often feared that it showed.

"Look," she tried to explain, searching for words that Royce would understand. "I realize charity events are good ways of getting positive press and word of mouth, but my events are known for having heart."

"Good. Then you can give a heart to mine."

She was still unsure how to make him understand

that this wasn't a good fit for her. To her relief, his phone rang.

"Yes, Matthew?" he asked over the speaker.

"I'm sorry to bother you, sir, but your lawyer just had the agreement you requested delivered."

"I need to take a quick look at this," Royce explained to Jasmine. "Excuse me a moment."

"No problem." A few minutes to herself might give her time to regroup.

Glancing around his office, Jasmine noticed right off that there were no personal touches. No novels or magazines. No photographs of his family...or even of him with friends. A framed photo of a large building graced a prominent spot on the wall.

Jasmine couldn't imagine being this impersonal. She knew a lot of people, cared about a lot of people, but her family was her core support. Few others got to see behind her public persona. After losing her parents when she was a teenager, she couldn't imagine the devastation she would feel if she lost any other members of her family.

She'd known Royce wanted an event planned—after all, that's what she did. But his complete lack of personal interest or passion was daunting. And though there were some charities that didn't require the benefactor to be very involved, it wasn't the way she wanted to work.

But how could she convince him that a more hands-on approach was needed?

"So what do you say?" The smooth smile on Royce's face as he returned to the room was so attractive it made her chest ache. She saw a lot of powerful, pretty men in her job, but Royce had to be the pinnacle. Frankly, she wasn't sure what to do with that, either.

"Should we start talking contracts?"

Jasmine nodded, willing her expression to remain neutral. "Yes, but I have a few requirements of my own."

Royce Brazier eyed the woman before him with concern itching at his brain, though he was too smart to let it show.

Jasmine didn't seem like the bargaining type. She appeared to be nothing like the cutthroat business people he dealt with on a daily basis. So why did he detect a hint of steel in those cornflower-blue eyes?

"A bit unusual for the event planner to start making demands, isn't it?"

She arched her brow in a challenging expression, but judging from the way she was tightly clasping her hands in her lap, he had a feeling it was false bravado.

"It's definitely not my normal MO," she said. "But a girl's got to have standards."

No apology—he liked that. "Name your price."

"Oh, it's not about price." She paused for a moment as she studied him. "It's about participation."

Royce was so caught up in her beauty that he wasn't getting all the cues. "I'm not following…"

"I'll happily take on your event—I already have some great ideas. And don't get me wrong. Being given a lot of freedom is an event planner's dream. But as I said, I have certain standards. This isn't about what's easiest for me…or you. A contract will require you to participate in each step of the process—"

"I guess we could touch base via phone." Though seeing her wouldn't be a hardship. Those blue eyes and her delicate bone structure were the first things to distract Royce from his business in a long, long time.

"You will participate by attending all the meetings that I deem necessary with vendors and representatives of the charity we support."

What? Hold on a minute. "Nice try, sweetheart. I have a business to run. And more than enough to do. That's why I'm hiring someone else to do this."

"I also have a business to run. And a reputation to protect. You need to be involved for this to work. So it's my way or no way."

Royce scrambled to figure out just what was going on here. "There's plenty of other event planners in this city."

Jasmine nodded graciously, but he again got the feeling there was steel behind the genteel smile. "And you're welcome to contact any of them, but they won't have the experience *I* have with your target audience." All too soon she was up and across the room, but she paused by the door. How could just the way she glanced back at him be so sexy? Especially as she proceeded to drop a bombshell. "I would like to remind you that I do know the Jeffersons personally, and I am a frequent guest at their parties."

Shock rocketed through him. How had she known?

"You *were* referring to the Jeffersons, weren't you? I do my homework, too."

As she strode out the door with a tempting flash of leg, Royce was impressed even though he knew he shouldn't be. *Sexy and smart.* It gave her too much of an advantage.

Two

"He knew exactly what he wanted," Jasmine told her sisters, "and he wasn't backing down."

"He's never come up against you before," Willow said with a grin. Jasmine's middle sister was a tenacious Southern woman, with the temper to match her copper-colored hair. Jasmine possessed a core of the same stuff but it only made a quiet appearance when necessary. She wouldn't scream and cry, but she didn't give up until every hope had been squashed flat by a steel-toed boot.

She might look like a lady, but she had more strength than most men. The tragedies in her life had demanded it. "Well, I believe I left him with some food for thought."

"So, you were wearing your blue dress?"

Jasmine frowned. Her sister's guess hit a little too close to home. "I didn't wear the dress to entice him. It's perfectly presentable."

Her sisters shared a grin. Jasmine tried to let it go. After all, she knew more than most that a little cleavage helped smooth the path she traveled. She'd be a fool not to take advantage of her God-given assets—especially when they'd helped her put both of her little sisters through college—in a completely respectable manner.

"Well, maybe the dress helped a little…" she admitted in a low voice as Auntie stepped into the kitchen with Rosie. The sight of her adopted daughter, and being surrounded by the people who meant the most to her in the world, filled Jasmine's heart and pushed aside thoughts of today's tedious meeting.

She reached out for six-month-old Rosie. She was in her snuggly jammies, her skin lavender-scented from her bath. As she settled into Jasmine's lap, Jasmine breathed deep. "I love you, baby girl," she whispered against Rosie's curly black hair.

Then she smiled up at the older woman. "Thank you, Auntie."

"You're most welcome," Auntie said, bending to hug Jasmine and the baby together.

Jasmine would never have made it through the first six months of Rosie's life without Auntie. Technically, she wasn't their aunt. She'd been their mother's nanny when she'd been small. She'd returned to Savannah when their mother hadn't needed her anymore.

But when the girls' parents had died, leaving them

with no family at a very young age, Auntie had brought them home to Savannah. Jasmine had been a young teen, but her sisters were even younger. Auntie had finished raising them in this house and never once complained. She was as close to a mother as she could get without being a blood relation.

Each of the girls loved her just the same.

Jasmine's baby sister, Ivy, joined them at the table with a plate of oatmeal cookies Auntie had made while they were all at work that day. "I've seen Royce Brazier at some of the meetings of the transportation planning commission, since he owns one of the biggest shipping companies on the East Coast," she said, her bright blue eyes wide. "He's pretty hunky."

Jasmine could practically see every set of ears around the table perk up.

Ivy continued, "But I've heard he's all business, 24/7."

Jasmine agreed. "He made that very clear."

Willow pouted. "What's the fun in that?"

"Dealing with demands is a lot easier when they're pretty," Ivy said, with a grimace that still managed to look cute.

Jasmine threw her napkin across the table at her sister, making a sleepy Rosie giggle.

"The last thing I have time for right now is a man," Jasmine insisted.

Her cell phone gave a quiet chirp, which was the ringtone she used at home so she didn't accidentally wake the baby. She glanced at the screen. "He certainly is a workaholic," she mused as she handed Rosie over to her youngest sister. She hadn't expected to see Royce's name on the caller ID at this time of night— or at all, really. She'd assumed he would never go for her conditions. Which had made her sad, because she could have used the work. But she had her principles.

She needed to remember that.

"This is Jasmine," she answered, walking toward the door to the front parlor as her sisters mimed something and Auntie watched them indulgently.

"Brazier here."

She smiled. *I know.* "What can I do for you?"

"After careful consideration, I've decided to renegotiate our terms, if that's still possible."

Interesting. "May I ask why?"

"Well, you certainly have a lot to offer."

Was she just imagining his voice growing deeper?

He went on. "So I'll agree to your terms—within reason."

"Meaning?"

"I'll attend meetings with the charity and vendors and such, but I'm not decorating rooms or tying bows or stuffing bags. Understood?"

Good thing he couldn't see her smile. "Feel free to email me your demands and I'll consider them."

"You can't talk now?" he asked.

"Roy—Mr. Brazier. It's a little late. Almost nine o'clock." And Rosie would need to go to sleep soon.

"Is your husband impatient for you to get off the phone?"

Okay, no way had she imagined that change in tone. Choosing to ignore his question, because it was fun to keep him guessing, she countered, "Don't you have a family waiting for you to shut down?"

"No. A man with my schedule shouldn't have a family—it isn't fair to them."

She thought of the little girl in the other room—how sometimes it was hard to force herself out the door in the morning because being away from Rosie left her feeling incomplete. Of course, life hadn't afforded her the chance to stay home with Rosie—and there were plenty of family members in the house to keep her occupied until Mommy came home. "Commendable of you to realize that." Though most men usually didn't think that way.

"Simply practical—but you didn't answer my question."

And she didn't plan to... "Working 24/7 isn't good for anyone."

"You enjoy your beauty sleep?"

This conversation was definitely off the business track—her brain derailed into forbidden thoughts of him in her bed. "I'll watch for your email," she said, hoping she didn't sound too breathless.

She disconnected and returned to the other room. Her sisters were silent until she tried to pass, then they started in.

"Oh, Royce," Ivy said, gasping with an extra dash of drama. "I must, simply must, have your email."

"Is your wife waiting for you to get off the phone?" Willow teased.

"He asked first," Jasmine protested.

"Which just gave you permission to dig."

"It's a business deal." Why did she have a feeling she was trying to convince herself?

"It doesn't have to be," Auntie said as Jasmine lifted a sleeping Rosie into her arms.

Jasmine lowered her voice. "Not you, too, Auntie."

"Your mother would not want you to be alone."

The sisters froze at Auntie's words. She rarely butted into their personal lives; though she was free with her help and guidance, her one very short marriage hadn't qualified her to give advice to the love-lorn—according to her. So this was rare.

"I'm not," Jasmine insisted. "I have you, the girls, Rosie. What do I need a man for?"

"I love the little one, too, and all you girls," Auntie said. "But you keep yourself tucked away, protected. Your mother, despite everything she lost, still pushed forward and allowed love in. She would want that for all of you."

Jasmine studied her sisters, who looked at each other slightly abashed. Theirs was a tight circle, and other than casual dates in high school and college, no man had ever infiltrated it. No man had even come home for dinner. And the sisters had always lived together, even through college.

They were their own island oasis. The thought of that changing sent a streak of unease through Jasmine.

As if reading her mind, Auntie nodded at her. "Keeping your circle small is not going to protect you from pain, Jasmine." She smiled sadly. "It's time, my sweets."

"For what?" Willow asked when no one else would.

Jasmine didn't want to know. Rosie was all the change she could handle in her safe little world. Her only challenges were in her career and she preferred to keep it that way. But when Auntie spoke in that all-knowing voice, things usually happened. Whether anyone wanted them to or not.

The older woman got up and crossed to the door. Jasmine could hear her progress up the stairs and eventually back down in the historic, but sturdy, home. Auntie came straight to Jasmine, leaving her with the feeling she'd been found by an unerringly accurate arrow.

Dropping into the chair next to her, Auntie held out a small jeweler's box. Willow and Ivy leaned across the table for a better look.

"Your mother wanted you girls to have this," Auntie said as she opened the box. "I found it with her things, packed away with a letter."

Inside lay a ring with a teardrop-shaped emerald stone surrounded by decorative gold filigree. They all gasped—Jasmine included. It was an involuntary reflex. The ring was gorgeous. Not only that, it seemed to have something…something special that Jasmine couldn't quite put her finger on.

"Wait!" Willow said. "I remember Mama wearing that—she said it was an heirloom or something…"

"Indeed," Auntie confirmed. "It was passed down to her from her mother, who received it from her mother, and so on."

Jasmine stared at the beautiful jewel, a sudden memory of it on her mother's hand filling her mind.

Her mother had been dressed up. An anniversary dinner, maybe? She and their father hadn't ever gone to fancy parties and such. About as fancy as it got was her father's Christmas gathering for the professors at the university where he taught. But she remembered her mother letting her stroke one small finger over the emerald. What had she said?

Then Auntie spoke, "Legend has it—"

Willow squealed. Jasmine groaned. Auntie gave them both an indulgent smile. Willow was the resident myth and legend hunter. She'd truly followed in their father's footsteps, teaching history at the local community college. She loved tall tales, mysteries and spooky stories. She propped her chin on her palm, avidly awaiting Auntie's words.

Jasmine just shook her head.

"Legend has it," Auntie started again, "that this ring was given to the woman who founded your family line by the man she married."

"Here in Savannah?" Ivy asked.

"Oh, yes. He was a pirate, you see, and she was the beautiful but shy daughter of a prominent family here."

Jasmine had tried hard to forget that their family had once been wealthy and respected. Long before the scandal that had rocked their safe little world.

Auntie went on. "He didn't think he had any chance to catch her eye, so he simply admired her from afar. But on his travels, he came into possession of this ring. He was told by the old man he bought it from that the ring would bring the person who owned it true love."

"Ooh," Willow said, her grin growing bigger and bigger.

"Sure enough, he was able to win his woman's hand…and the ring has been passed down to every generation of your family ever since. Each has claimed its power is real."

Ever the skeptic, Jasmine couldn't help but add, "And look how that worked for them. Scandals, death. Our family has some of the worst luck ever."

When Ivy's hopeful expression fell, it made Jasmine feel like a big bully.

"It's said to bring its owner true love, not an easy life," Auntie gently admonished, ever the voice of wisdom. "Besides, if the scandal hadn't driven your grandparents out of Savannah, then your mother and father might never have met."

Jasmine didn't want to disrespect the memory of her parents, but… "A ring did not cause them to find each other—being in the same place at the same time did."

"Maybe so—"

"Don't be a realist, Jasmine," Willow complained. "Embrace the magic."

Ivy reached over to take the sleeping baby and snuggled her close. Rosie gave a shuddering sigh. "Is it really healthy to teach Rosie that there's no magic, no romance in the world?"

"She's only six months old," Jasmine protested. "Besides, I didn't say that—" Jasmine created magic every day with her events, or rather, the *feeling* of magic.

Willow added her two cents' worth, even though

Jasmine considered her biased. "Yeah, Jasmine, haven't you ever heard of Cinderella? Rapunzel? Beauty? Wendy? Dorothy?"

"You want me to convince Rosie there's magic in the world by indulging this nonsense and snaring a man?"

"No—the man is just a bonus," Ivy said with a giggle.

"An uptight CEO?" Jasmine couldn't believe she was hearing this.

Ivy wasn't deterred. "The uptight CEO with thick hair, muscular build and a tight a—"

Willow gasped and covered the sleeping baby's ears. "Ivy!"

Ivy grimaced. "But yes—that is a bonus. You just need to sweeten him up a little."

"For Rosie?"

"Yes!" her sisters said in unison.

"She needs a man around," Ivy went on. "After all, we didn't have one. How can we possibly teach her anything about men?"

They all paused, silently weighing the loss of their father. The only man they could remember being part of their family...and that was a long, long time ago.

Auntie finally weighed in. "She's already going to hear enough reality when she gets older and learns what happened to her birth mother," she reminded Jasmine with a sad look.

"Or are you just afraid the ring will actually work?" Willow jumped in.

Was she? Jasmine secretly admitted that all the loss

she'd suffered in her young life made her reluctant to let someone else in. Only dire circumstances had brought Rosie to her. Jasmine had adopted her as a newborn at the behest of the little girl's dying mother. A woman Jasmine had come to know at the City Sanctuary mission where she'd volunteered—and then lost when Rosie's mother succumbed to the cancer she'd never been able to afford to have treated properly.

"The ring is for all of you girls, but I think Jasmine has a unique opportunity here to prove her point…or ours." Auntie held out the ring box once more, smiling as if she understood Jasmine's dilemma all too well. "A little magic never hurt anyone," she said.

Somehow, Jasmine didn't believe that.

Three

So much for that businesslike attitude. Jasmine tapped her stiletto heel as she glanced at her watch once more. *He's twenty minutes late.*

She knew traffic hadn't held him up. The coffee shop she'd chosen for her brainstorming meeting with Royce was right near his office building. As she watched the boats on the river and the tourists wander by on the sidewalk, she struggled with her impatience.

Yes, something probably came up: a business call, papers to sign, something.

But why hadn't someone called? She'd sent the contract in plenty of time. Her racing thoughts were driving her crazy.

I'll wait ten more minutes.

Just sitting here was annoying her all the more, so

she dumped her coffee and set off toward his office building.

The gorgeous architecture and sweet smell of pralines from a riverside candy shop didn't calm her agitation as she walked over the stone pathways. Tension built up inside—a problem she'd never had with her clients. What was it about this guy? Usually she could just breathe and reroute her focus to where it needed to go in order to produce forward momentum toward their mutual goals.

Not today.

Days spent wondering what that tattoo was on his neck, whether his hair was mussed when he rolled out of bed in the morning or if he ever did anything but work had taken her to places she hadn't wanted to go. And the stupid ring wasn't helping.

She glanced down at the emerald she wasn't used to having on her right hand. So stupid. But if she backed down now, her sisters would never let her hear the end of it. So she'd prove to them that the legend wasn't real—and teach Rosie there were plenty of special things in life without magic.

Her phone started vibrating in her hand. Glancing down, Jasmine mumbled under her breath, "Well, it's about time."

"Hello, Mr. Brazier," she said.

His tone was as clipped as hers. "I need to postpone. Please come to my office in an hour." He was so short, she wondered if he even realized he was talking to an actual person.

"Excuse me?"

"Come here in an hour," he repeated.

Click.

An hour? Jasmine paused to scroll through the calendar on her phone. *Oh, my.* Since Royce had only allotted an hour for their meeting, Jasmine hadn't worried about the tight timeline she had for this morning. An hour would put her right smack in the middle of Auntie's doctor's appointment. Willow was in class. Ivy was at work. Which left…well, no one to watch Rosie. Except her.

He probably wasn't going to like how that went… But then again, he hadn't really given her much choice in the matter. It was time Mr. Brazier got his first lesson in seeing the person behind the business opportunity.

When Jasmine walked into the outer office a little over an hour later, Matthew's eyes widened. "Miss Harden, I'm so sorry." His eyes widened further—if that was even possible—as he glanced down. "I—"

"Just announce me, please, Matthew," she said with an overly sweet smile.

Her stomach fluttered from the nerves rushing through her in waves, but she reminded herself necessity took this out of her hands. Besides, he'd brought it on himself.

Jasmine went through the door while Royce continued to talk on the phone. His back was to her. Taking advantage of his distraction, she turned and smiled down at her surprise. Then she lifted Rosie from her stroller and turned to find Royce staring at her backside.

Jasmine should have been offended, but his distraction played to her advantage in this instance. When he finally realized where he was staring and looked up, the switch from lust to shock in his normally schooled expression was priceless.

"What's this?" he sputtered as he jumped to his feet.

Jasmine ignored Rosie's cooing, because breaking her businesslike facade wouldn't be to her advantage right now. "You told me to meet you here."

He frowned, proving himself to be heartless. No one could look at Rosie and refuse to smile. No way could he be human. "My office isn't a day care," he insisted.

"And my time is very tightly scheduled today," she said with an arch of her brows. "I have commitments, just like you."

"I can't help that my earlier meeting ran over," he said defensively, straightening in his seat.

Jasmine took a deep breath, then blew it out slowly, pulling her chaotic thoughts from the last hour together. "Let me ask you a question," she began.

After Royce nodded, she continued. "Would you have called any of your fellow businessmen and given them commands about when to show up at your office?"

The surprise on his face only confirmed her suspicions.

"If I were one of your managers or the owner of one of your supply companies instead of an event planner, would you have had Matt contact me to reschedule instead of rudely cutting off our conversation earlier?"

"That's not why—"

"I made arrangements for a sitter as soon as this meeting was scheduled. I don't like to disrupt my daughter's schedule by carting her around to my business meetings. But by changing our scheduled time and refusing to discuss it with me or give me any options, I had no other choice…unless I wanted to be a no-show myself."

He didn't respond. His narrowed gaze still made her want to squirm, but she refused to back down.

"Now I'm very much looking forward to working with you, but my business is people. Is our phone conversation earlier how you conduct business? How you deal with your fellow business people and the community at large? Because it isn't how I conduct my business."

Lesson number one was over. The ball was in Royce's court now.

Rosie continued to coo, then snuggled against Jasmine as she settled into a chair with her child in her lap. This would never have worked if Rosie had a different temperament, but Jasmine happened to know that her daughter was one of the most easygoing babies in the world. She just hoped this was Royce's only lesson in seeing the people behind the business.

"If that's going to be a problem," she said, "then I release you from your contract right now."

He glanced back and forth between her and Rosie,

as if he still couldn't catch the connection between his earlier behavior and having a baby in his office. But then he slowly shook his head. "No. I don't want to cancel our contract."

She wanted to ask why, but figured she'd pushed her luck enough for today.

"Maybe we should reschedule?" Royce said, staring down at them with a frown.

"Why?" Jasmine asked. "I'm here now. Your schedule appears to be free at the moment, which it hasn't been for the last two weeks. Let's talk."

When he hesitated, she prompted. "If we don't get started soon, we'll miss your window of opportunity. I can't work miracles in two months. And neither can the vendors I hire."

Royce's careful expression returned as he took his seat. "I've found most people have a price that will motivate them."

"And that's the difference between the two of us."

Surprise momentarily replaced his serious expression. "What do you mean by that?"

"Just that I prefer to endear myself to people," she said, keeping her tone even and calm, not accusing. "I find they're much more willing to work hard, which makes life easier and the results quicker, if I'm nice."

"As opposed to employing coercion?" His smirk reminded her of exactly how they'd gotten into this situation.

"Sometimes other tactics are necessary," she conceded, "but it definitely makes things messy and uncomfortable for everyone. Confrontation might be a necessity at times, but I don't like it."

They shared a look of mutual understanding. Royce agreed with a nod. "But it is interesting."

Interesting, indeed.

Royce studied the woman in front of him, carefully avoiding looking at the raven-haired child in her lap. The sight of the little girl in his office brought too many mixed emotions.

He'd never been so far off his game that he wasn't sure where to begin…until this moment. But he wasn't about to let Jasmine Harden know that. She was proving her point…he wasn't about to help her.

For a moment, he second-guessed his decision to continue with this conversation. Heck, this whole project. But it wasn't just her connection to the Jeffersons that kept him from calling a halt right now.

Deep down, as uncomfortable as this entire incident made him, his instincts told him a woman who was this passionate about people was perfect to create the event that would connect him to others who were just as passionate.

"So, what do you have for me?" he finally asked.

The twitch of her lips suggested she knew exactly how uncomfortable he was. She shifted the baby into the crook of her arm with the ease of an earth mother, despite her power suit, and started her pitch.

"I want to do a masquerade."

Masquerade? "Like a dance?"

A half smile formed on her elegant red lips. Why

did they have to be shaped so perfectly? He'd promised himself he would keep his thoughts on business...not on the woman. And he'd succeeded until the minute he'd seen her in person again.

Then she'd had to insist on him seeing her as a person. This wasn't helping him with his perspective at all.

"Sort of. A masquerade includes dancing. The key focus is the anonymity. Each participant wears a mask, which lends itself to a mysterious atmosphere."

"Isn't the point for people to know me?" He had to admit, he wasn't an imaginative kind of guy. At least, not in this area. Give him a logistics problem with his shipping company and his brain went into overdrive. Fantasy? Not really.

"Oh, they will," she assured him. "There will be announcements throughout the evening of the money being raised so everyone will be aware of the sponsor. But for the *participants*, the atmosphere is key."

She reached into her oversize bag to pull out a tablet. Flipping the cover open, she deftly pulled up what she was looking for. "As you can see, this gives us a theme to work with—a theme our target audience will find very attractive."

Without missing a beat, she set the device upright on his desk and flipped through pictures on the screen of lavish decorations and food and costumes. The only thing Royce saw were dollar signs.

"This looks awfully expensive."

Jasmine raised her brows at him. "Is money a problem?"

How could she make him feel like a schoolboy with a single look? "It isn't unlimited," he insisted.

"I wouldn't think so, but you said you wanted to make an impression."

Royce studied the last photo. A woman in a fitted dress and feather mask was laughing up at a man in a black tux. The woman's dark hair reminded him of Jasmine's… No—she was an employee. An employee with a baby.

Totally off limits.

"Why can't we just do a dinner?" he asked.

Of course, she had to counter with, "Why would anyone want to come?"

He studied the picture, realizing how totally out of his element he was. Maybe she'd been right to get him more involved. He had no idea how to attract people to anything other than a business deal.

"The draw at a charitable event isn't even the charity," she said, "which is a shame, but true."

A shuffling sound had him looking up. The baby's chubby cheeks and pale round face surrounded by a halo of inky black hair made her look like a cherub. She stared at him with her eyelids at half mast, thumb firmly held between her lips. When had the cooing stopped?

Jasmine leaned over to reach into the back of the stroller. When she straightened, she held a bottle that the baby eagerly reached for. Royce couldn't help but notice that there wasn't a ring on Jasmine's ring finger. No wedding band? He should have been even more upset by this situation, given his own childhood. Instead, a relief he was ashamed of snaked through him.

The fact that she was available shouldn't matter to him.

Settling back into the chair, Jasmine cuddled the sleepy child against her chest. The juxtaposition of working woman and mother unsettled him. His own mother had never seemed that at ease. Royce had always felt like he hindered her work whenever he was around.

"People want to be entertained," Jasmine said. "You have to sell an experience in order to get people to show up and spend their money. Build something that intrigues them and they'll tell all their friends and soon you'll have people begging for tickets."

The brief flicker of her thick lashes as she looked down at the dozing child in her lap had him holding his breath until she looked back up. But then she narrowed her gaze on him, giving him the uncomfortable feeling that she saw more than he wanted her to. "The more people who talk about wanting to attend, the more likely the buzz will get back to the Jeffersons. The name connected to the event matches the name on the newest bid they received. Mission accomplished—or at least you'll have made progress."

Royce was far more comfortable talking strategy than entertainment. "I wondered how we would make that connection."

She seemed to pull the baby a touch closer in her arms. He didn't want to notice, didn't want to think about the child. Royce had never attended a business meeting that gave rise to this many emotions—unease, lust, surprise, irritation. How long until this meeting was over?

"Besides being the talk of the town?" she asked. Her smile turned as mysterious as the woman in the photograph. "I may have a few tricks up my sleeve. After all, we need to get the word out in certain circles...so I thought I would use a few exclusive invitations I receive to introduce you around, talk it up."

"You want me to make social appearances...with you?" As if social appearances weren't awkward enough for him.

She nodded. "Including at the Jeffersons' Sunday Salon."

"You get invited?" So, she hadn't been exaggerating when she'd claimed a connection.

"About every other month."

The Sunday Salon was a coveted invite that didn't come around that often for most people. The Jeffersons must adore Jasmine Harden, which told Royce he'd made the right choice of event planner—even if he didn't feel all that comfortable with it.

"All right," he said. "Tell me more."

He couldn't complain that Jasmine wasn't thorough. In ten minutes, he knew more than he really wanted to, but he had no doubt she was the best woman for the job. Before she finished he was convinced she would oversee every detail and nothing would be missed. She addressed every aspect of the planning, including quite a few things he never would have thought about.

"So what do you think?" she asked.

A lot of things he couldn't say at the moment—because they were completely unbusinesslike. Luckily she wasn't looking at him as she efficiently laid the baby down in the stroller. Was it terrible of him that he didn't know the child's name and was afraid to ask?

"Sounds good," he said, eager to be away from all the churning thoughts this meeting had raised. "Send the mock-up and budget projections to Matthew. Let me know when you need me for anything."

Her brows rose at his short tone, but she didn't question him. "I'll do that." She gathered her bag and tablet, then faced him once more. "When you look at the budget, remember that successful events involve getting all the details right, and that takes a lot of people."

"While logically I understand that—" and he truly was getting on board with the concept "—I still have to look at the bottom line."

Jasmine stared at him a moment; he detected the barest hint of an eye roll before her thick lashes swooped down. "Let's put it this way—is the time and money worth it to gain the new contract?"

Her words registered, but instead of thinking about business, Royce found himself holding his breath, waiting to see if she would look back up and show him those intense blue eyes once more. Then the baby let out a big sigh and broke the spell.

As Jasmine leaned over to look into the stroller, he forcibly pulled himself back to reality—and the knowledge that this woman was off limits in more ways than one.

"Yes, it is," he said. "You may proceed."

"Okay—we will need to start with the charity."

"I've told you it doesn't matter to me. Pick whatever you want."

"I have. You'll be helping raise money for a new building for the City Sanctuary homeless mission."

Royce nodded even as he tuned her out—though it wasn't as easy as he would have liked. He didn't care about the details—didn't want to care. He also didn't want to care about her thick hair and expressive face or the curves highlighted by the black power suit she wore.

"Also, we need to pick a venue right away. What dates would work for viewing possible locations?"

Her sharpened tone caused Royce to snap back to attention. She hadn't been kidding about the participation thing. Her long stare reinforced her message.

"Check with Matthew. He'll know what's available."

Smartly she stood up and pointed the stroller toward the door.

Royce had the sudden conviction that he couldn't let her walk out the door without making himself clear, as well. "I realize my point of view isn't a popular one these days, but as the child of a hardworking single mother myself, I have a strong opinion about children in the workplace," he said.

Glancing back at him, she asked, "What's that?"

"My office isn't a day care but I do apologize for my rudeness on the phone."

She gifted him with a sexy smile that had no place in his office, as much as he wished it did. But then came the sass. "Remember that and we will work together just fine."

Before he could respond, she pushed the stroller out the door. He heard her tell Matthew goodbye with that same sweet tone—this time with no steel undercurrents. She was definitely infuriating and intriguing.

Thoroughly dangerous territory.

Four

He'd thought about not showing up at all.

Staring up at the austere lines of the museum Jasmine had chosen as a possible venue, he wished he had ditched their meeting. But standing her up again was not a good option. She'd taught him that much.

Besides, his mama would have considered it ungentlemanly to simply ditch her—even if memories of his mama were what made him not want to show up at the museum in the first place.

But he had to stand firm. Today, he would take back the reins because he would not hold his event in a building he could no longer set foot in—much less play host in for an evening.

He was still staring at the building when Jasmine

pulled up beside him in a pristine compact sedan. After climbing out, she smiled at him.

"Well, look at you," she said, her voice as teasing as it had been that first night on the phone when he'd called her. He didn't like to acknowledge the tingles of anticipation that hit him when he heard it—which were just as strong this morning as they had been then.

"I was a little unsure that you'd actually show up," she went on, "much less arrive early."

The tingle of anticipation grew, only this time it was for the challenge he knew was ahead of him. Still he struggled to keep any emotion from his expression.

"There's no point in going inside," he said, letting his tone match what he hoped was his deadpan expression.

Her frown as she shut the door and walked around the front of her car warned him that she was thinking hard about this turn of events. "May I ask why?"

"We aren't having my event here."

She glanced back over her shoulder at the building behind her, the multiple columns majestically holding up the austere gabled roof with its carved marble depiction of birds. When she turned to him, confusion reigned in those gorgeous blue eyes. "Again, may I ask why?"

"I don't want it here." And he didn't. No need for discussion about his troubled childhood or dead mother. "Personal reasons."

"Are they good enough reasons?" she asked, tossing her hair over her shoulder.

"It is when I'm signing the checks."

Her expression told him she wanted to be offended, even when she knew he was right. But she wasn't simply accepting his decree. "I thought you didn't want to be involved in the decisions?" she demanded.

This wasn't the same as dealing with any of his other business associates. When they slapped their hands to their hips, he never noticed the sway of their breasts. He shouldn't be noticing Jasmine's now, but somehow he couldn't help himself.

"And you said you wanted me to be involved in making the decisions," he reminded her. "Which is it?"

That little intake of air pushed her breasts out just a touch more. Heaven help him.

She nodded. He could tell she wanted further explanation. He wasn't giving it.

Finally she turned away, giving him a break from that penetrating gaze. "Let me go touch base with the manager," she said. "I need to stay on good terms here."

"Of course."

"Then we'll talk," she warned. Her heels clicked on the sidewalk as she strode away.

He waited until she went inside the museum before pulling out his phone. "Hey, Joseph," he said when his construction manager picked up. "How are things looking today?"

Joseph filled him in on the details of the kitchen installation at Royce's supersecret project, as well as other aspects of the restoration.

"Another day on track," Joseph confirmed.

"Good."

Royce hung up, a spur-of-the-moment idea buzzing in his brain. He had the lucky ability to run through all the immediate pros and cons of a decision in a relatively short amount of time. This had helped him jump on opportunities that other businesses spent months preparing for. Along with his intense drive, he'd used this to build his business to magnificent proportions at a very young age.

Today this ability would certainly come in handy.

He waited until Jasmine returned down the walk fifteen minutes later. His relief at finally being able to leave the site of one of his most traumatic childhood experiences was tempered with his desire to covertly take her in.

Jasmine seemed to enjoy ultrafeminine clothing. Even when she'd had the baby with her, she'd been wearing a women's business suit with a skirt and an undershirt with lace lining the deep V of the collar. Today, the bodice of her navy dress hugged curves that he normally wouldn't notice. But on her they made his mouth water. An inverted triangle cut out over her cleavage added to the effect. The flowing skirt that ended right below her knees revealed just enough of her legs to be tantalizing.

Was she trying to torture him?

"All done," she said as she approached. "What now?"

Oh, she was gonna love this. "I have an alternative. Let's go."

"Now?" Her frown was back.

"No time like the present. I'll drive."

But as they settled into the small space of his luxury sedan and the dark, sexy scent of her snuck up on him, he had to wonder whether he had made a wise choice.

Or was this self-sabotage?

Of all the things Jasmine had expected to do today, riding in the front seat of Royce's car was not one of them. The smooth, heavy scent of well-cared-for leather and a slight hint of aftershave teased her senses, making her notice things she wished she didn't.

This is business. This is business.

"Why don't you have a driver?" she asked, letting the first question that occurred to her pop out in an awkward attempt at conversation.

He glanced her way before returning his attention to the road. "That's a rather pretentious question, don't you think?"

"Actually it's simple curiosity that springs from experience," she corrected. "I've worked with a lot of Savannah's upper class. Most have their own drivers—at least, under certain circumstances."

The road was familiar to her from having lived in Savannah since she was fifteen years old. Though a lot of fine old houses could be found in the surrounding areas, she couldn't think of any in this particular direction. Where was he taking her?

She tempered her curiosity with more questions about his driverless state. If she had to be thrown off her game plan for the morning, at least she could work toward finding the human behind the robot. "You're the youngest billionaire in Savannah," she reminded him. "Heck, the entire South. Doesn't a driver come with that title?"

"That title came with a lot of hard work. Besides, I love to drive."

"So you're human?"

His locked-down tone surprised her. "More than you know."

Great. Her curiosity was growing like an overinflated balloon. Pretty soon she might explode from it—but that was better than drooling over his blond good looks.

"Why won't you share those personal reasons with me?"

She wasn't sure why she asked. Maybe to get herself away from her attraction to Royce. Maybe to dig deeper into the mysteries she had begun to see. If she hadn't been watching his face, she'd have missed the flicker of surprise that appeared on his expression before he shut back down.

"I told you, I don't want to talk about it."

He had, but that wouldn't stop her from trying. "Sometimes it helps."

"Not true."

Stubborn man. "Have you ever even tried?" She suspected not, considering that he seemed like the all-business-all-the-time type.

She could tell her question annoyed him by the way he tightened his hands on the steering wheel. "We're almost there," he said, instead of answering.

Fine.

Then Jasmine looked around, realizing exactly how

far out of town they were. Uneasiness started to grow deep inside. "You realize that the farther we are from town, the less likely people are to attend the event, right?"

"Oh, they'll show up for this."

His confident tone didn't turn her into a believer—after all, she was the expert in this business.

The minute he turned down a particular driveway, her fears were confirmed. She'd only been down this driveway once. A very long time ago, and only by accident. Later when she'd started researching the place, she'd realized what it was. They could not have their event here.

"Royce, no." Her grip on the seat tightened as tension took hold of her. "We can't do this here. Do you know how long Keller House has been empty?"

"It was empty for over twenty years," he said. "The carriage house has been occupied for five years. It's currently the home of the caretaker."

Okay, so maybe she didn't know everything. "But the main house must be in need of hundreds of thousands of dollars of renovations."

"Four hundred thousand in renovations, to be exact," Royce said. She swore she could hear a smirk in his voice. "And that doesn't include the back gardens, which can't be started on until closer to spring."

She eyed him suspiciously as he pulled the car to a halt before the front steps. He looked back with perfect calm, so she turned her attention to the house. The massive gray stone building seemed sad and silent from where she sat. "And how do you know that, Royce?"

He ignored her as he exited the vehicle. She stared up at the imposing edifice, waiting for him to come around to open her door. When he did, she got out and stood in the space between the door and the car to look him straight in the eye.

"I can't oversee renovations while I'm doing an event," she said. "And what owner in the middle of renovations would want an event here?"

"No, the renovations are my job. The event is yours," he said, enunciating clearly. "Just get out of the car."

I've gone from dealing with a difficult boss to biting off more than I can chew. Jasmine stepped away from the car and stood before the mammoth building. It was gorgeous, even in its rundown state. Ivy climbed up one corner. Though cracked in a few places, the gray stone still lent a majesty to the structure. Even the steps were made of it. She could imagine women walking up them in huge hoop skirts on their way to a ball here.

"I've always been curious about this place," she said. "My sister, who is a big history buff, says that the Kellers used to be the most prominent family in Savannah. Their house was detailed in many newspaper accounts and gossip columns throughout the years. But then the entire family was wiped out by smallpox."

"Shall we go inside?" he asked.

She met his gaze. "You're serious about this?"

"I am. We will hold the masquerade here."

She glanced between him and the house that hadn't been a home to anyone in a long time. He'd gone from uninvolved to highly involved more quickly than she could wrap her brain around. "So you are a bit of a philanthropist," she said.

"No. Real estate is a good investment."

But as he turned away she glimpsed something in his expression. Something he probably didn't want her to see. She had a feeling that like the building before her, he was hiding an awful lot behind that facade of his.

Five

Just a quick walk through to see the current state of renovations, let Jasmine take a quick peek and then they'd head back to the city. That was Royce's plan, and, by damn, he was sticking to it this time.

But it wasn't helping that he found her caution amusing as she stepped through the massive antique double doors. Clearly, she expected the inside of Keller House to be a disaster.

Granted, the exterior still needed work, but there was plenty of time to get to that. The exterior would be a years-long project, just as the inside had been. And the craggy, cracked surface had character that Royce kind of enjoyed.

The wonder on her face as she took in the already renovated foyer made his heart speed up. Royce quickly looked away. *No distractions. Focus.* He had a feeling her enthusiasm, in addition to being attractive, would be infectious.

But he was here for business.

As per his usual MO, he mentally identified what he needed to do. Then he started purposefully down the main hallway that cut the house virtually in half. The kitchen lay at the other end, which was where he hoped to find his construction crew hard at work.

"Wow! Is this staircase the original? Or a reproduction?"

Royce froze. "It's the original," he conceded, then moved a few more steps. Maybe if he kept moving, she would follow.

Her gorgeous blue eyes were roving up and down the magnificent two-story structure. "It's beautiful," she breathed. "Who did the renovations?"

He took a few more steps, even though she hadn't budged. "Jasmine, I don't have much time to get this done, so if we could move on—"

She nodded and moved to follow, though her gaze stayed glued to the refinished mahogany and blue tile patterns along the edges of the steps. He turned away and picked up speed. His brain started to produce a list of all the things he needed to discuss with the foreman.

"All these tiles…are they Italian?"

Royce heard the question but kept moving.

At first he thought he heard her following, but then the footsteps stopped and her voice sounded farther away. Royce paused, glancing over his shoulder. No